THE ART OF ACCIDENTS

Twenty-one days with Charvaka Guru

Charvaka Philosophy of Pure reason

Dr. Anshuman Telang

Title: *The Art of Accidents*
Author: Dr Anshuman Telang

First Edition: 2000

ISBN: 978-93-344-0500-2

Published by: Anshuman Telang
[contact author: +91 9532864747]
[Varanasi, India]

Printed in India. This is a work of creative philosophy.

While inspired by historical figures and traditions, the dialogues are reconstructed imaginatively by the author to explore the scientific and philosophical idea of survival.

Dedication

For the children of Earth.

You were not born to follow,
but to see, to ask, to learn.

Do not be trapped by promises of another world.
Only this life is everything you have.

Live with open eyes and a questioning mind.
That is the only truth worth keeping.

May you see that life is not a gift from the heavens,
but a flame lit by chance, carried forward by survival.

And

May you learn to live not in fear of accidents,
but in wonder at the art they create.

Preface

There is no other idea in this world to which I am as deeply attached as the idea of **survival**.

Survival is not just a struggle of the body, it is the hidden thread that runs through all of life. It shapes the forests and the Nature, the animals and the humans, it shapes our earth and some day it would shape the whole universe.

It shapes our emotions, our logic, even the very illusions of our minds.

To me, survival is the **artist** that has painted the canvas of nature and continues to carve the form of every living being.

It is by chance that life exists, by chance that it continues, and by chance that it has taken the form we see today. This chance, this accident, has been the true sculptor of life.

The word accident comes from Latin root *accidens* which means "to happen, to occur, to fall upon”. It means something that befalls you unexpectedly.

Nevertheless, there are several other meanings too, for example:

Unintended Event or Random Occurrence, something that happens without intention, not always bad.

In philosophy, an *accident* is a property, which may or may not belong to a subject without affecting its essence. For Example: *Colour is an accident of a flower; its essence is being a plant.*

Thus, accident is not always a tragedy. It is also chance, possibility, and the unexpected shape of things.

The word *art* comes from the Latin *ars*, meaning *skill, craft, method*. Its root is the Proto-Indo-European *ar- meaning to fit together, to join*. From this root, art grew to mean:

Art is Skill in making, in shaping, in creating with intention. Art is the practice of beauty, imagination, and expression.

Art is a craft, a method, even a system of rules for doing something well.

Art, then, is both skill and expression, craft and beauty the deliberate act of shaping. And when it is not deliberate it can be called as an accidental art.

Life is the art of accidents and genetic mutations are those tiny accidents that happened in billions and zillions of times in different ways to create this beauty, that we call life or nature.

"Survival is an accidental artist and the Life is the art of accidents."

This book is written under the belief that everything we see is **The Art of Accidents**.

The way chance has, through survival, created forms, feelings, families, and even the longing of the human mind to go beyond death.

Dr Anshuman Telang

Prologue

There are names that echo through history not because they were written in books, but because they refused to bend before the weight of tradition.

Among such names is **Brihaspati**, remembered not for scriptures he composed, but for the doubt, he planted in the minds of men.

The strange fate of this thinker is that he himself left no words behind. Not a single verse, not a single sutra can be traced directly to his hand.

And yet, for centuries, sages and philosophers could not stop speaking of him. He was remembered because he was criticized.

The sharpness of his thought cut so deeply that others, even those who opposed him, had to preserve his voice in order to strike at it.

Thus his memory survived not through devotion, but through conflict, like a flame kept alive by those who tried to blow it out.

In the generations that followed, the name *Brihaspati* became more than a man. It became a title, carried by those who sat at the head of the Charvaka ashram.

The guru was no longer one figure but a continuing presence, a torchbearer of the philosophy that dared to say,

"Look at the earth beneath your feet, not the heavens above your head. Trust what your eyes see, not what unseen gods demand."

This philosophy, "Charvaka Darshan", was not built on worship, but on observation.

It did not seek to save a soul for the afterlife; it sought to understand the body, the senses, the world of flesh and soil and sky. Its roots were not in prayers, but in questions. Its strength was not in rituals, but in reason.

Later disciples, wishing to preserve the fragments of their master's thought, wrote the Brihaspati Sutras. Much of it has been lost, yet enough remains to remind us of a voice that was both rational and daring.

At that same time, in another corner of the land, a prince was born. His father was a king, proud, stern, and aware that his son must one day rule.

For this reason, the boy was not sent only to warriors to learn the bow, or to priests to learn the hymns. He was sent to seek wisdom from every great teacher of the age.

The king believed, *"A ruler must hear not only the voices of those who agree, but also the voices of those who challenge. A king who hears only blessings becomes blind. A king who hears criticism becomes wise."*

Thus, one part of the prince's training was to be spent at the ashram of the Charvaka guru.

For twenty-one days, the young prince sat with Brihaspati. The ashram was no palace; it was simple, earthy, often cold in the winter winds.

There were no grand temples, no golden statues, and no hands rising to the heavens. Instead, there were only questions and answers, words sharpened like arrows, yet carrying the warmth of fire.

Each morning, afternoon, or night, the disciple and guru spoke. Sometimes they sat under the fog, sometimes in the rain, sometimes in the glow of firewood at night. The rhythm of nature itself seemed to guide their lessons.

The conversations were not about gods or heavens. They were talking about life. About survival. About why the body hungers, why the mind imagines, why fear grips us, why love holds us, why families form, why societies rise, why beliefs cling, and why even the idea of the soul may be the mind's desperate trick to avoid death.

There is a paradox here. The guru who wrote nothing gave a prince a gift that could not be written down but could shape a lifetime.

For the prince, these twenty-one days were not just education. They were a mirror, held before his mind.

Would he return to his kingdom to rule as a king, carrying these insights into the art of survival?

Would he choose instead to remain a seeker, an ordinary man walking the path of questions?

Or would he find a way to be both, a ruler outside, but a philosopher within?

This book is a retelling of those days, of dialogues that may have vanished into the winds, but which still hold truth even now. For survival is not an ancient truth, nor a modern one. It is the truth. The law that shapes not only nature, but thought itself.

Survival is an accidental artist. Life is an art painted by accidents, by chance, by the unpredictable weaving of time and space.

And it is this art **, the *Art of Accidents*** that you will witness in the pages that follow.

The *Art of Accidents*

Twenty-one days with Charvaka Guru

1. The Accidental Spark, how survival emerged from random mutations and chance in evolution

2. The Struggle for Existence, natural selection, and survival instinct that shaped us

3. Extinction. The Forgotten Majority, Lessons from the countless species that did not survive

4. The Survival Instinct, from invisible organisms to humans: the will to persist

5. The Body as a Survival Machine, Hunger, thirst, sleep, and immunity

6. The Brain: An Organ for Survival, Why logic, memory, and learning evolved

7. Fear and Emotion, How love, anger, sadness, and joy protect survival

8. Sex and Reproduction, Ensuring survival beyond the self

9. Family Bonds, Kinship as nature's insurance

Day 1

The Accidental Spark

It was a cold December morning.

The sun was weak, hiding behind the fog, and the air felt sharp on the skin.

In the grove of Sal trees, two people sat facing each other.

One was young Gautam, the disciple, and the other was Brihaspati, the Charvaka teacher.

Gautam sat on a mat of grass.

He wore a simple cotton dhoti and a thin shawl, which he pulled tightly around his body to fight the cold.

His breath came out in small white clouds.

His face showed both the pain of the winter and the eagerness of a student waiting for answers.

Brihaspati sat straight and calm.

He wore a thicker woollen cloth wrapped around his body. His face was strong and still, not showing any discomfort.

His eyes looked sharp, and his voice carried slowly but clearly in the quiet forest.

“Master,” Gautam said softly, shivering a little, “you have told me that life was not made by the gods.”

“Then tell me, how did life begin? How are we here today?”

Brihaspati’s eyes did not move. He said, “Do not call it a miracle, Gautam. Life began not with purpose, but by chance.”

“Long ago, the earth was full of storms, smoke, fire, and oceans of boiling water. In that great chaos, some tiny pieces of matter joined together in a special way.”

Gautam leaned forward, his lips pale, his shawl slipping. “What way, Master?”

“The first sparks of life,” Brihaspati said slowly.

“They were only small invisibly tiny parts of nature (molecules), not alive like us, but they could make copies of themselves.”

“When they copied, sometimes they made mistakes (Mutations). Many mistakes destroyed themselves.

"However, some mistakes made them stronger. No god helped them. Only chance. Only accident. That is how survival began."

Gautam's eyes grew wide. His lips trembled as he asked, "So life itself was born from mistakes?"

Brihaspati gave a faint smile. "Yes. From mistakes, from chance, from chaos. Most forms vanished. A few stayed. They grew, they changed, and they survived."

"Life is not the rule of the universe".

"It is the rare exception. Countless worlds are empty and silent. But here, by accident, the spark caught. From it came you, me, every tree, every bird, and every thought."

Gautam looked down at the cold earth. His toes were numb, his breath heavy. The forest felt bigger now, and its silence deeper. The truth of his master's words pressed on him more than the winter chill.

Brihaspati placed a strong hand on his shoulder. "Remember this, Gautam . No God made these laws of survival. Survival is not a gift from heaven".

"Survival is an accident."

“And those living beings who accidently held on these survival laws, survived. Others got extinct.”

Gautam lifted his eyes again. His face showed both fear and wonder.

Wrapped in his thin shawl, he felt smaller, yet also freer.

He had begun to see the world as it truly was.

Day 2

The Struggle for Existence

The winter sun was higher today, but the chill still hung in the air. The fog had begun to lift, and the grove of Sal trees looked brighter.

Birds moved from branch to branch, shaking the dew from the leaves.

Gautam sat close to Brihaspati, still wrapped in his thin shawl. His eyes were full of questions, and his face showed the thirst of a mind that could not rest until it found an answer.

"Master," Gautam said, his voice calm but curious, "yesterday you told me life began by accident."

"But why do some animals live and others die out?"

"Why do we see so many different creatures, some strong, some weak, some beautiful, some full of flaws?"

Brihaspati looked at him carefully, his hand resting on his wooden stick, his favourite staff.

"Gautam, life is not protected by gods"

"The world itself decides which forms remain and which disappear."

'Every creature struggles to live, to eat, to grow, to have children. In this struggle, some are able to survive, and others cannot. That is the way of nature."

Gautam frowned, his breath showing in the cold air. "So, Master, it is not goodness or fairness that decides? It is not gods who make the rules?"

Brihaspati shook his head. "No."

"Look at the deer and the tiger. The deer runs fast, but the tiger is strong. Both fight to survive. Sometimes the deer escapes, sometimes the tiger eats. There is no hand of god that saves one and kills the other. It is the chance of nature, the test of strength, speed, and cleverness."

"The one who fits best in his place lives longer and leaves more children. Those who do not fit, slowly disappear."

Gautam's eyes grew wide. "So the world itself selects? Nature is like a judge?"

The teacher's face softened, but his voice stayed steady. "Yes and when you say this, you are just naming things as person, nature is not a person and that is why you can observe that nature is no fair judge."

"It has no kindness, no cruelty. It only allows those who can survive to continue. And remember, Gautam, survival is not about perfection."

"If the world were made by gods, would they give us sickness, weakness, hunger, and pain?"

"These are signs that life was shaped not by design, but by struggle."

"Nature keeps both strengths and flaws."

"That is why in every tree, every bird, every man, you will find both good and bad."

Gautam pulled his shawl tighter. His young face showed both confusion and wonder.

"So, Master," he whispered,

"the beauty I see in the peacock's feathers, the sharp claws of the tiger, even the bent back of an old man, all are nature's way of shaping survival?"

Brihaspati nodded. "Yes."

"The struggle for existence makes every form what it is."

Some live for a time, some vanish forever. This is how the earth writes its story".

"Not by divine will, but by the endless test of survival."

The disciple lowered his gaze to the soil.

He traced lines with his finger, as if trying to draw meaning from the earth itself.

Around them the forest carried on, full of calls, cries, hunts, escapes, a great struggle happening everywhere, unseen yet unbroken.

And in that moment Gautam felt the truth.

Life was not a gift to be kept safe, but a battle that never ends.

Day 3

Extinction, The Forgotten Majority

The sun rose weakly through the winter haze, sending pale beams through the bunch of a few Sal trees.

The frost still clung to the grass, shining like tiny crystals. Birds called in the distance, and the smoke from small village fires mixed with the morning air.

Gautam sat on his mat, his thin shawl wrapped tightly around his shoulders. His eyes were sharp, and his face carried the weight of yesterday's lessons. He was ready for more.

Brihaspati arrived slowly, his woolen wrap hanging heavy but neat, his wooden stick tapping the ground as he walked. He settled onto the earth with steady grace.

His eyes, calm and deep, turned toward his disciple. "Today, Gautam," he said, "we shall speak of those who are no longer here."

Gautam's face tightened with surprise. "The dead, Master?"

Brihaspati shook his head slightly. "Not just the dead, but the forgotten. For every living creature you see, the crow, the cow, the fish in the pond, there are thousands of kinds that once lived but live no more. They are gone, lost to time. Extinct."

The disciple shivered, not only from the cold.

"But Master, if life continues, why would so many vanish?"

His brows knit together, and his lips pressed as though holding back fear.

"Because survival is not promised,"

Brihaspati said firmly. "The world is harsh. Fire, flood, hunger, cold, the teeth of stronger animals, all are waiting. If a form cannot endure these trials, it disappears."

"Remember, Gautam, what you see around you is only a small part of what once lived. Most creatures lost the struggle."

Gautam's eyes grew wide, his voice low. "So, Master, the world is full of graves we cannot see?"

Brihaspati leaned forward, his stick pressing into the ground. “Yes. The earth is covered by silence that once was full of sound.”

“Huge animals greater than elephants, birds bigger than peacocks, creatures stranger than any we know, all gone.”

“And yet, from their loss, others found space to grow. Nature does not keep everything. It forgets. That forgetting is called extinction.”

The disciple bent his head, his breath coming slowly. He traced a shape in the ground with his finger, a circle that broke as the wet earth stick to his finger.

His young face showed sadness mixed with awe. “Master,” he whispered, “then we too may one day vanish?”

Brihaspati’s face held no pity, only truth.

“Yes, Gautam. Man is no exception. Just as many before us vanished, so may we.”

“This is the law of nature, most will not survive. What you see is not the full story of life, but only the survivors’ tale.”

"The earth remembers the winners, and forgets the countless fallen."

The forest fell quiet.

The mist was lifting, and the call of a distant bird echoed in the cold morning air.

Gautam raised his eyes, his face pale yet shining with a strange fire.

For the first time, he felt the weight of all that had been lost, and he understood that survival was not common, but a very rare event.

And everything alive today stood on the bones of the forgotten majority.

Day 4

The Survival Instinct

That afternoon the winter sun was brighter, and the chill was less sharp than the past days.

A soft breeze moved through the Sal trees, carrying the smell of dry leaves and distant wood smoke.

Gautam sat waiting, his shawl loose this time, for the air no longer bit at his skin. Yet his face showed worry.

The guru was late. He shifted on his mat, his fingers fidgeting with the edge of the cloth.

A thought troubled him, Is Master unwell?

At last Brihaspati appeared, walking slowly with his favourite wooden stick. His face looked the same, steady, unbent, yet his late arrival had left the boy restless.

He bowed as the guru sat down. "Master," Gautam asked softly, "are you sick? You came so late today."

Brihaspati gave a small smile, the lines of his face calm.

"No, Gautam. Sometimes we walk slowly and time runs fast, especially when our mind is heavy with thoughts. Nevertheless, I am here now."

"Today we speak of survival itself, the will to live that runs through all beings."

The boy leaned forward, his eyes bright with relief. "The will to live, Master?"

"Yes," Brihaspati said.

"From the very beginning, life has fought to stay alive. We may not know the shapes of the first beings, for they were too simple and too small for our eyes."

"Reason tells us this, before the tiger and the peacock, before the fish and the trees, there must have been simpler forms."

"Small, with only the most basic powers , to take food, to grow, to divide into two. From such small beginnings came all the richness we see today."

Gautam's lips parted in wonder. "So, Master, the world began not with large and perfect beings, but with the smallest and weakest?"

Brihaspati nodded.

"Yes. Great trees rise from tiny seeds. So too life rose from the simplest sparks."

"These small beings did not know beauty or wisdom. They knew only how to cling to existence."

"That is the root of survival , a drive so deep it shapes every living thing. Even now, the smallest worm turns to save itself, the smallest bird fights to feed its young."

"The instinct to live is the oldest law of life."

The disciple lowered his gaze, his hand pressing against the soft green grass on the earth. His young face showed both calm and fire, as if he had touched a truth too large to hold.

"So, Master," he whispered, "all our actions, eating, running, building, even thinking, come from this will to survive?"

Brihaspati leaned on his stick and looked at him closely. "Yes, Gautam. Every hunger, every fear, every joy, all are servants of survival."

"Life began with the smallest and the simplest. Over time, it grew more complex, cleverer. However, the root remains the same, the will to continue, to persist, to hold on. That is survival."

The Sal grove was quiet in the afternoon light. A crow called in the distance, and the air felt softer than the past cold days.

Gautam breathed deeply, his shoulders easing, yet his mind burned with thought.

He now saw life not as a gift, but as a chain , starting from the smallest and simplest, pulled forward only by the will to survive.

Day 5

The Body as a Survival Instrument

The morning sky was heavy with clouds, and soon the rain came, soft at first, then stronger. Drops fell through the Sal leaves, turning the earth dark and wet.

Gautam and Brihaspati had no choice but to walk to the nearby cow shelter. There, under the palm leaf roof, the two sat on low wooden planks, while cows stood around them, their breath warm and their tails swishing.

The smell was strong, but in the guru's ashram, that smell was seen as sacred, a reminder of life and giving. Still, the cows moved often, their hooves knocking against the floor, their low sounds breaking the silence of the lesson.

Gautam wrinkled his nose at first, but then folded his hands, steadying himself.

Brihaspati's eyes caught the boy's unease, and with a slight smile he said, "Do not let the cows trouble your mind, Gautam. Even their bodies are part of today's lesson."

"For we will speak of the body, the great Yantra (machine) of survival."

The disciple straightened eager to listen. Rain drummed on the roof, mixing with the soft grunts of the cows.

Brihaspati began, his voice calm and deep. "Think, Gautam. Why do we feel hunger?"

"So that we may eat, Master, and live," the boy replied quickly.

"Good. And thirst?"

"To drink, and live."

"And sleep?"

"To rest, Master, so that the body may rise again with strength."

The guru nodded. "Yes. Hunger, thirst, sleep, even pain, all are not punishments but tools. They guide the body to act so that it may continue."

"This body is like a chariot made by nature. The bones are its frame, the muscles its ropes, the heart its drum, the stomach its fire. Each part has one task, to keep life going."

A cow bent close, sniffing at Gautam's shawl, making him jump back a little.

The guru chuckled. “Even this cow feels the same forces. It eats, drinks, rests, and fights sickness. Its body too is a survival instrument.”

Gautam, calming himself, whispered, “So every ache, every hunger, every breath, they all serve one master, survival?”

“Exactly,” said Brihaspati. “When you bleed, the blood thickens to seal the wound. When fever rises, the heat burns away harm.”

“When eyes close at night, the body heals itself in silence.”

“All these powers live in us not for comfort, but for survival.”

“Remember, Gautam, the body is not built for beauty or perfection. It is built to last, to endure.”

The disciple lowered his head, his face thoughtful.

The cows stirred again, one letting out a loud call that echoed in the shelter. Gautam smiled faintly this time. “Even the cows remind us, Master. Their bodies too work in the same law.”

The guru placed his palm on his cross folded knees. His eyes shone in the dim cow shelter.

"Yes, my child. From worm to cow to man, the body is nature's tool. A Yantra (machine) of survival. Nothing more, nothing less."

Outside, the rain softened, but the air was still heavy with the smell of dung and wet earth.

In that sacred shelter, among beasts and men alike, Gautam felt he had touched another truth, that life itself was a body's long fight to go on.

Day 6

The Brain, An Organ for Survival

In India, the month of December is like the mood of a beautiful girl, shifting and full of surprises.

Some days are rainy and soft, some bright and golden with sunlight, others heavy with fog, and some cloudy and dull, as if the sky itself has grown sad.

That day, the air was strange. Morning passed into afternoon, and Gautam sat waiting under the trees, his eyes fixed on the path from which his guru always came.

But the hours dragged, and Brihaspati did not appear. The boy's heart grew restless. He walked to the pond, then back again, and then sat staring at the red ants carrying grain.

Evening began to fall, and still the teacher had not arrived.

At last, as the sky turned violet and the first stars showed, Brihaspati's figure came slowly along the path.

Gautam rose quickly, relief mixing with a small hurt. He bowed low. "Master, I waited all day. Why so late?"

The guru rested his staff on the ground and looked at the boy with calm eyes. "Patience, Gautam. Some lessons ripen only with waiting."

"Today we speak of the brain, the crown of the body, and yet only another servant of survival."

They sat near a small lamp, its flame trembling in the evening air. A cow lowed in the distance, and the sounds of night insects began to rise.

Brihaspati began, his tone firm. "Tell me, Gautam. Why do you remember the path back to your hut?"

"So that I may not be lost, Master."

"And why do you learn words, numbers, chants?"

“So that I may use them when needed.”

The guru nodded. “Yes. Memory, thought, even speech, all are tools.”

“The brain is no different from the stomach or the lungs. It has one purpose, to keep you alive.”

It stores paths so you may find food and shelter. It remembers faces so you may know friend from foe. It learns skills so you may work and survive.”

Gautam’s brows drew together. “But Master, what of great thoughts, of poetry, of wisdom? Are they too for survival?”

Brihaspati’s lips curved into a slight smile. “Even poetry, Gautam. When a man sings, he wins love. Isn’t it for survival in a different way? Species survival?

“When a leader speaks with wisdom, he binds people together. When a thinker plans, he protects his tribe. The brain makes beauty and reason, but beneath all of it lies the same law, survival.”

The boy’s eyes widened. “So the brain is not a gift of the gods, but a tool of nature?”

“Exactly,” said Brihaspati. “It is like a torch in the dark.”

"Human mind is not given by gods; it is shaped slowly, sharpened by the struggles of life itself."

"Without the brain, no beast or man could last long. It is the organ of survival."

The flame of the lamp flickered, and Gautam's face shone in its glow. His heart was full, though his mind trembled with the weight of this thought.

The evening sky deepened, and the first chill of night touched the Charvaka guru's Ashram.

Yet inside him, a new warmth grew, the knowledge that even the highest powers of man, his very mind, were but servants of the same ancient will, the will to survive.

Day 6

Lessons continued during night hours

The Longing Beyond Death

The evening lesson had ended, yet the night was still alive. Godhuli fire (Dusk fire) was the ritual of ashram, under the open sky, its flames rising and falling in the cold air.

The stars stretched wide above them, clear and endless, and the chill of December crept into the earth.

Gautam and Brihaspati sat close to the fire, their shawls pulled tight.

The cows had long fallen quiet, and only the crackle of burning wood broke the silence.

Gautam's face was lit by the orange glow.

His eyes were restless, as if something within him refused to be still.

At last he spoke softly, almost with hesitation. "Master, if you forgive me, I want to ask a question."

Brihaspati turned his head, the firelight dancing in his calm eyes. A faint smile touched his lips.

He always loved when students refused to remain silent, when their hunger for truth became stronger than fear. "Ask, Gautam. Tonight, the fire is bright and my ears are open."

The boy leaned forward, his voice trembling between doubt and daring. "You said the brain is only for survival?"

"But Master, if that is true, why does the mind fear death so deeply?"

"Why does it long for something beyond death? I feel, and I have seen others feel, that men want to live forever."

"Is not all of spirituality born from this longing? That the brain, knowing death cannot be escaped, invents a survival beyond death?"

"Is this not the root of man's misery?"

The Guru's smile deepened, though his eyes grew heavy with thought.

He held the end of his stick near the fire, watching the sparks rise into the night. "Ah, Gautam, you pierce where it hurts."

"Yes, the brain knows death is certain."

"And because it is evolved, to help the body to survive, it cannot bear this truth, that despite all its efforts, death is inevitable".

"So it dreams. It builds heavens, rebirths, eternal souls.

All these are the brain's last struggle, its attempt to survive even when the body must fall."

Gautam's eyes shone, though his brow was furrowed.

"Then, Master, is all our religion, our hope, our prayers, only a trick of the brain?"

Brihaspati looked up at the stars.

His face was calm, his breath steady. “A trick, perhaps, but a powerful one. When men believe they will live again, they gather courage.”

“They face battles, pain, loss. They endure.

Belief itself becomes another tool of survival.

“Do you see, Gautam? Even the dream of immortality serves life.”

The disciple was dumbfounded, he lowered his gaze, his hands pressed together, torn between awe and unease.

“So the misery of man, his fear of death is also his strength?”

“Yes,” the guru said, voice low and firm.

“It is both. Misery and strength. Curse and blessing.”

“Man knows he will die, and probably this same knowledge makes him create songs, build temples, love deeply, and dream of forever.”

“The fear of death is the shadow that shapes the fire of life.”

The flames flickered high, sending sparks into the black sky.

Gautam's young face glowed with both fear and wonder, as if he had glimpsed a truth too vast to hold.

Brihaspati leaned back, his shawl tight around his shoulders, his smile faint but full.

In the stillness of the cold December night, the fire burned.

And so did the thought, that even beyond death, survival ruled the human mind.

Day 7

Fear and Emotion, Guards of Survival

The next morning, Gautam rose early as always, but he did not expect his guru to come soon.

The night before had stretched long, their talk burning as bright as the firewood, and he knew Brihaspati would rest late.

By the time the sun was already climbing, the group of Sal trees was still cool, and the clouds floated heavy across the sky.

In hot months, clouds are like gifts, softening the fierce sun. But in the chill of December, they hang low and grey, pressing the spirit down.

Gautam thought to himself, Strange, how the same cloud can be joy or burden.

That is how humans are too, never one thing, but always shifting.

When at last the sound of the guru's stick touched his ears, Gautam looked up with calm expectation.

Brihaspati came slowly, his shawl wrapped close, his face unreadable.

Gautam bowed, but there was already a question burning in his heart, ready before the guru even sat down.

The teacher rested under the tree, his back straight, his eyes soft with thought.

"Today," he said, "we will speak of fear, and of those emotions that rule you when reason cannot."

Gautam leaned forward eagerly.

"Master, are emotions too only for survival? Even fear, even love?"

Brihaspati's lips curved in a half-smile.

"Think, Gautam. When the deer runs at the sound of a twig, what is it?"

"Fear, Master."

"And when a mother guards her child with her life, what is it?"

"Love."

"Then tell me, are these not the same as teeth or claws?"

"Nature's weapons, only softer, hidden inside the heart?"

Gautam's eyes grew wide.

He had never thought of it this way. "So emotions are not weaknesses?"

"Not at all." said Brihaspati firmly.

"All the positive and even negative emotions are there to empower us"

"They are shields. Fear keeps you from walking into danger."

"Anger gives you strength to fight when reason says you cannot win."

"Sadness binds you to those you lose, so you do not forget them and so others may hold you".

"And joy tells you when life is safe, when survival is flowing well."

The boy's face brightened as if a light had been lit within him.

Yet another doubt rose. "But Master, emotions often mislead us. A man may fear shadows that are not real. A man may love one who harms him. Why would nature give us such flaws?"

Brihaspati gazed at the clouds, their shapes drifting like restless spirits.

His voice was slow and deep.

"Because nature is not perfect, Gautam. It is not a god with a plan."

Nature is a blind weaver, making mistakes and beauty together.

"Fear saves many, but it also fools some. Love binds families, but it can also chain a man to sorrow. Still, without them, no man would have survived at all."

The cold wind stirred, carrying the smell of wet earth from the rains of the past days.

Gautam sat silently, feeling both small and strong.

For the first time, he saw his own emotions not as a burden, but as companions, silent guards walking beside him on the path of life.

The guru looked at his disciple with quiet pride. “Remember, Gautam.”

“Your thoughts may guide your steps, but it is your emotions that keep you alive.”

And with that, the morning lesson ended, leaving the clouds to drift and the boy to sit still, his heart echoing with the truth that survival itself had shaped even the deepest feelings of his soul.

Day 8

Sex and Reproduction, Survival beyond the Self

The next dawn was wrapped in fog. The trees, the huts, even the cows in the shelter looked like shadows in white smoke.

The air was so cold that each breath came out like mist, and Gautam rubbed his hands together, waiting for his guru. He had slept little, for his mind was restless after the last lesson.

When Brihaspati appeared through the fog, his figure looked almost like a ghost, slowly becoming clear as he came closer.

He sat down on the damp ground, wrapped tightly in his shawl, his face calm as always.

"Today, Gautam," he said, his voice steady in the cold, "we speak of the oldest drive of life, sex and reproduction. Tell me, why do you think living beings join together in this way?"

Gautam thought for a while. "To give birth to children, Master."

"To make sure life continues."

The guru nodded. "Yes. Without food, you would die. Without water, you would die. But without children, your line, your kind, your people would vanish. Reproduction is survival, only not of one body, but of the chain that links past to future."

Gautam's brow tightened. "But Master, why is it so powerful in men and animals alike? Why does it drive them so strongly?"

"Because," Brihaspati said softly, "nature has no pity for the weak or the careless. If living beings did not burn with desire, they might forget to join. And if they forgot, their kind would end. So nature gave this hunger, as strong as hunger for food, so life would not stop."

"And what about people of other genders, why nature created them" Gautam tried to puzzle his guru.

"Seems like you forgot that analogy, Gautam, nature is like a blind weaver" Charvaka guru was calm.

The fog thickened for a moment, and only their voices seemed to move in the still air.

"But Master," Gautam asked again, "if this is true, then even love is not some divine gift, but only survival?"

Brihaspati's eyes gleamed. "Love, desire, bonding, yes, they all rise from the same root."

"When two people feel joy in each other's presence, when they hold each other close, when they raise children together, that too is nature's trick to guard survival."

"Without such feelings, parents might abandon their young, and the child would die."

So even love is survival in disguise.

The boy was flabbergasted. His face showed both wonder and doubt. "Then, Master… is there nothing pure in it? Nothing beyond survival?"

The guru smiled, not mocking but gentle. "Does it make it less pure, Gautam, to know its root?"

"A tree grows from mud, yet its flower is still beautiful. So it is with love and desire. Their base may be survival, but the song they sing in the heart is still sweet."

The fog began to lift slowly, and the morning sun pushed through in pale light.

Gautam looked at the clearing sky and felt a quiet stirring inside, half understanding, half mystery.

The guru's words echoed in him, survival beyond the self.

Beyond individual survival, there is species survival.

And so the lesson ended, leaving the disciple to wonder if perhaps the will to live was not only in the body, but in every bond that tied one life to another.

Day 9

Family Bonds, Kinship as Nature's Insurance

The morning was heavy with fog. The sky was a dull sheet of grey, and no bird dared to sing. Gautam sat close to the dying fire, blowing on his hands to keep them warm.

The stillness felt strange, no rustle of leaves, no sound of wings. He whispered to himself, "God knows where birds hide in such cold, depressing seasons."

Soon he heard the soft sound of footsteps in the wet grass. The guru appeared, his shawl wrapped tight, his face calm, though the cold seemed to bite everyone else.

He sat down without a word, only closing his eyes for a moment as if listening to the silence itself.

"Gautam," he began slowly, "yesterday we spoke of reproduction, and how life survives beyond one body.

“Now listen carefully, survival does not stop with birth. The newborn is weak. Alone, it would die. So nature gave another bond, the family.”

Gautam leaned forward, eager. “You mean the way parents care for their children?”

“Yes,” Brihaspati said, his breath misting in the air.

“A mother’s milk, a father’s protection, the closeness of blood ties, these are not gifts of gods, but tools of survival.”

“Think, Gautam: why would a mother endure pain to give birth, and then risk her life again to guard her young? Why would animals fight till death for their offspring? Because if they did not, their line would end.”

The fog seemed to grow heavier, muffling the world around them.

Gautam’s face was thoughtful. “But Master, family is not only parents and children. Brothers, sisters, uncles, aunts, they all stand together. Why?”

Brihaspati’s eyes brightened. “Because blood is nature’s chain. Even if one link breaks, another carries it forward.”

"When you help your brother, you are really helping your own blood to survive. When you defend your cousin, you are protecting a piece of yourself."

"This is why families hold together. Not out of pure kindness, but out of the deep law of survival."

Gautam frowned slightly. "Then love for family is not selfless?"

The guru smiled gently. "Does it need to be selfless to be true? Survival writes its law in our bones, and yet it feels like love, duty, care. That feeling is what makes it real. If there were no love, families would break, and the weak would perish."

"So love is survival, but survival dressed in beauty."

The silence of the morning deepened, only the sound of their breaths in the cold air.

Gautam looked out into the fog, where no bird sang, and thought of his own parents, his kin.

He felt a warmth in his chest despite the bitter cold.

"Master," he whispered, "so family is nature's insurance, to make sure life does not fail."

Brihaspati nodded slowly. "Yes, Gautam. Blood guards blood. In this, nature is wise."

The fire crackled faintly, the only sound in that silent morning, as if even the earth was listening to the old truth.

Day 10

Friendship and Tribe. Why Alliances Mattered More than Isolation

The sun had broken through at last. The heavy fog of past days melted away, and the noon light poured golden on the ashram courtyard.

The earth, damp and shining, gave off a soft smell, and the trees seemed to stretch happily toward the warmth.

Birds, missing for days, fluttered and chirped as if celebrating their return.

Gautam sat cross-legged, his face lifted toward the sun, letting the warmth soak into his chilled body.

He smiled without meaning to. "Today feels like life itself has woken up, Master."

Brihaspati, arriving with his slow, steady steps, nodded. "Yes, Gautam. Nature teaches even through the weather.

Alone, one cannot push away the cold fog. But when the sun joins, everything changes."

"Just as one man alone is weak, but with friends, with a tribe, he grows strong."

Gautam straightened, attentive. "You mean, survival is not only about family?"

The guru lowered himself to the ground, the folds of his shawl catching the light. "Yes. Family is the root, but not enough."

"Think of the hunter. Alone, he may starve or be killed by a wild beast. But with a group, one watches, one hunts, one guards, one carries the kill. Together they live. Together they scare away danger."

The birds chirped louder as if echoing his words.

Gautam's eyes lit with understanding. "So friendship, tribe, community, they are survival too?"

Brihaspati's lips curved in a small smile. "Exactly.

Even the animals know this. Wolves hunt in packs, monkeys warn each other of danger, ants build homes together."

"Man is no different. His heart seeks friendship because his body needs protection. His mind longs for belonging because without it, he is exposed".

"Solitude may sound noble, but survival is rarely found in isolation."

Gautam's brow creased slightly. "But Master, friendship feels so warm, so joyful. Is it only survival wearing another mask?"

The guru's gaze was steady.

"Tell me, Gautam, is it any less true because it is evolved for survival? The joy of companionship is not a lie. It is the way survival becomes sweet."

"Nature is clever, she makes what is needed also feel good. That is why men gather, why they share food, why they laugh together under the stars."

"Alone, a man may live a little while. Together, a people live for ages."

The noon air was alive now, filled with the chatter of birds and the distant sound of children playing.

Gautam breathed deeply, his heart lighter than on the foggy days before. He understood, friendship was not only comfort; it was the shield of survival.

Brihaspati lifted his hand toward the bright sky. “Remember this, Gautam. The tribe is the armor of man. Without it, he is naked in the wilderness.”

Day 11

Society and Civilization, Large-Scale Cooperation as Survival Strategy

The dawn was pale, still half-asleep, with a faint line of pink stretching across the eastern sky. The village around the ashram had already begun to stir.

Thin smoke rose from the huts as women lit their morning fires, and the faint, rhythmic sound of a conch echoed from a distant temple.

The smell of burning cow dung cakes mixed with the cool air, sharp yet strangely comforting.

Gautam wrapped his shawl tightly, his breath misting in the cold. His eyes followed the faint figures of villagers carrying water pots, their voices low, their steps steady.

He turned as Brihaspati appeared, the soft crunch of his sandals on the earth announcing his arrival.

"Master," Gautam said softly, "these mornings feel alive with people. The whole village wakes together, moves together. It feels powerful."

Brihaspati sat beside him, his face calm, his eyes reflecting the faint light of dawn. "And therein lies man's greatest strength, Gautam."

"Alone, even the bravest man is fragile. But when thousands move with a single rhythm, they become unshakable."

Gautam tilted his head, curious. "You mean society itself is a tool of survival?"

The guru nodded. "Yes. Think, Gautam. Families give birth to children. Tribes give safety and warmth".

"But society?"

"society builds roads, temples, wells, and walls. It creates rules so that men do not kill each other but live side by side."

"Civilization is nothing but survival written on a larger canvas."

The sound of cattle bells drifted in as herds were taken to the fields.

Brihaspati pointed toward them. "See there? One man alone cannot tame the land. But with many, fields are ploughed, food is stored, armies are raised."

"Even knowledge, Gautam, it survives not in one head, but in scrolls, in songs, in the memories of thousands."

Gautam's brow furrowed. "But Master, if all this is survival, why do we also see cruelty, war, and oppression in society?"

Brihaspati sighed, his breath visible in the cold. "Because survival is not gentle. Just as the forest has both shade and beasts, society too has both order and cruelty.

The same strength that builds also conquers. The same rules that protect one group may crush another.

"Civilization is not perfection, Gautam, it is only a greater chance to endure."

Gautam lowered his gaze, he was in deep thinking mode, the truth was heavy yet clear.

The faint sun finally broke through, painting the horizon with a golden glow.

Brihaspati's voice grew firm."Never forget."

"Society is man's shield and his prison, his pride and his burden."

"But above all, it is his path to survive, longer and stronger than he ever could alone."

The conch sounded again, louder now, as if sealing the lesson with its echo.

Day 12

Religion and Belief, Survival through Shared Myths and Meaning

The evening was quiet and heavy with mist. Gautam and Brihaspati walked slowly to the riverbank, where the air smelled of wet earth and burning oil lamps.

Villagers had gathered there, placing little clay diyas on the water. The flickering flames floated downstream, dancing like a trail of fireflies.

From the temple on the far side, soft chants rose and mingled with the sound of flowing water.

Gautam's eyes lingered on the lamps. "Master," he said softly, "these lights look so beautiful, but why do people do this? Why do they worship the river, the stones, the sky? Is it truly for gods, or something else?"

Brihaspati sat on a smooth rock, his shawl wrapped tight around his shoulders.

His face glowed faintly from the firelight. "Gautam, men create gods not because they see them, but because they need them."

"Alone, a man is weak. But when hundreds bow before the same fire, the same stone, they are bound together. Belief becomes the rope that ties them."

Gautam frowned, looking at the chanting crowd. "So religion is not truth, it is for survival?"

The guru's eyes softened. "Yes."

"Myths are not built for heaven, they are built for earth."

"They teach people how to live, what to fear, whom to obey, and why to endure. Even false stories can keep a village united, can stop bloodshed, can give meaning to suffering."

"And meaning, Gautam, is a powerful tool for survival."

A cold breeze blew, making the lamps shiver on the water. Gautam pulled his cloth tighter. "But Master, what of those who question? Who do not believe?"

Brihaspati looked into the river, the reflection of the flames dancing in his eyes. "Those who question may stand alone."

"But remember, Gautam, the crowd survives longer than the lone man."

"Religion is not about gods, it is about togetherness".

"When men share a story, they share a strength greater than their own."

The chants grew louder, echoing across the dark water. Villagers pressed their palms together, their faces glowing with faith.

For a moment, Gautam felt their unity, a strange warmth, as though the entire village breathed as one body.

Brihaspati's voice broke the silence. "Do not mistake belief for truth."

"Yet do not ignore its power".

“A myth can outlive kingdoms, a prayer can outlast swords. For survival, even illusions can be real.”

The last lamp drifted far, its flame trembling before the mist swallowed it. Gautam watched it vanish, a shiver running down his spine.

Day 13

The Illusion of Free Will, Are Choices Just Survival Scripts?

The fog had finally lifted. After many days of gray skies, the morning broke bright and clear, though the air was sharp with biting cold.

The sun rose like a golden coin above the trees, spreading a thin warmth that did little against the chill. Frost or probably dewdrops still clung to the grass, shining like glass.

Gautam stood outside the ashram, rubbing his hands together for heat. He felt lighter today, the sight of the sun after long gloom filled him with a quiet joy.

Soon, the steady sound of footsteps came, Brihaspati, walking with slow grace, his shawl heavy around his shoulders, his breath visible in the cold air.

“Master,” Gautam began eagerly as the guru sat upon the flat stone, “yesterday you spoke of belief. You said myths tie men together.”

“But today I wish to ask about choice. We often feel, when we act, that it is we, who decide. That freedom belongs to us.”

“Is this true, that we have free will or is it also another illusion?”

Brihaspati smiled faintly, his hand resting on his knee. The sunlight touched his face, revealing lines of age and wisdom. “Ah, Gautam, men love the thought of freedom. It flatters them. But the truth is harder.”

“Look at the crow above us. It chooses to fly toward the grain field. Is that choice, or hunger leading it?”

“Look at the cows in the yard. They move toward the hay. Is that free will, or need?”

“And tell me, when you chose to come to me, was it not thirst for knowledge that pushed you?”

Gautam lowered his eyes, thinking deeply.

"So you mean, our choices are not free, but driven by something beneath us?"

The guru nodded slowly. "Yes. Hunger, fear, desire, love, all push us like hidden hands. The mind is proud, it says, 'I chose.' But beneath, nature whispers, 'I made you choose.'

"This is why I call free will an illusion. What we call freedom is often only survival speaking through us."

A flock of birds passed overhead, their wings beating against the cold sky. Gautam followed them with his gaze, his face troubled. "But Master, if all is decided by nature, then are we nothing more than puppets?"

"Is our whole life only a script written for survival?"

Brihaspati looked at him kindly, the sun shining behind his head like a halo.

"Yes and no. We are bound by the needs of survival, yet within those limits, we shape patterns".

"A farmer cannot command the sun or the rain, but he can choose how to plant, when to sow, how to care for his crop.'

"That is the narrow field where man walks, between necessity and possibility."

Gautam's lips parted as if to speak, then closed again.

His brow furrowed, a shadow of unease crossing his face.

The guru leaned forward, his voice softer, like the warmth of the morning sun breaking the cold.

"Do not be disheartened".

"Even if freedom is small, it is still precious."

"Like a flame in a storm, it may be weak, but it can still give light. Remember, Gautam, illusions, too, are part of survival."

"The belief in free will gives man courage to act."

And sometimes, courage itself shapes destiny."

The crow cawed loudly and flew into the distance.

The sound echoed in the clear sky.

Gautam looked at his master with new eyes.

Realizing that even in chains of survival, man's spirit sought wings.

Day 14

The Pursuit of Happiness, Joy as a Signal of Survival Success

The afternoon was warmer than the mornings had been. The sun sat high, spilling golden light on the fields where children played and women washed clothes by the stream.

The winter air was still cool, but a soft breeze carried the smell of baked rotis from village huts. The sky was open and blue, and after many gray days, even the smallest things seemed to glow with life.

Gautam waited under the shade of a Peepal (fig) tree outside the ashram. He felt a kind of calm joy in his chest just watching the simple scene of village life.

When Brihaspati arrived, his shawl lighter than usual, Gautam greeted him with folded hands and a bright smile.

"Master," Gautam said, "I have been thinking about what you said yesterday, that even free will is shaped by survival. But what about happiness?"

"Why is it that when we laugh, when we feel joy, the world seems right? Is happiness itself also tied to survival?"

The guru settled himself on the stone seat, closing his eyes for a moment as though feeling the sun's warmth.

Then he opened them, his face calm. "Yes, Gautam. Happiness is not a mystery gift from the gods. It is nature's way of guiding us."

"When you eat after hunger, you feel joy. When you find shelter on a cold night, you feel peace. When you win the love of a friend or family, your heart grows light. Do you see?"

Happiness is a signal, it tells the living being, 'What you did was good for survival.'"

Gautam tilted his head, listening carefully. "So even joy is like a message from within us? Like fire gives light, our body gives happiness to show the right path?"

"Exactly," Brihaspati said, his voice gentle.

"It is nature's reward. A child laughs when his mother embraces him, because safety is survival."

"A man smiles when he wins respect, because respect brings allies. Even the peasant sings at harvest, because grain means life through the winter. Joy is not separate from survival, it is the shining face of survival."

Gautam's eyes widened with wonder.

He looked at the children playing with sticks in the dust, their laughter rising into the air. "Then even this laughter, their happiness, it is not wasted? It has meaning?"

The guru's lips curved into a faint smile. "Yes, Gautam. Nothing in life is wasted. Every tear, every laugh, is part of the great script."

"Happiness tells us we are on the path of life".

"Sorrow tells us to beware, to change. Both are tools of survival."

"But remember, man is clever."

He learns to chase joy even when survival is not in danger. That is why he makes music, art, festivals.

"He stretches the feeling of life beyond hunger and shelter. In this lies both his beauty and his folly."

The afternoon sun grew warmer, and a mild drowsiness spread in the air. Gautam sat quietly, his face peaceful, as though the words had sunk deep into his heart.

For a moment, he felt that happiness itself was sitting beside him, like an invisible friend.

Day 15

The Fear of Death, How Mortality Shapes Culture, Art, and Morality

The winter had returned with its sharp teeth. That morning, a cruel cold wind blew from the north, filling the air with mist.

The fields lay empty and silent, as if even the birds had withdrawn into some secret shelter.

Gautam pulled his woolen shawl tighter around his shoulders as he walked to the ashram. His breath came out in small clouds, vanishing quickly into the fog.

When Brihaspati arrived, his step was slower than usual. He lowered himself onto the stone seat, the mist curling around him like a white veil.

For a long time, he said nothing. The silence itself felt heavy, like the earth holding its breath.

Finally, Gautam spoke, his voice low.

“Master, yesterday you told me that joy is nature’s signal of survival.”

"But I see another thing in man's heart, a shadow. A fear that never leaves. It is the fear of death."

"Why does this fear live in us always, like a ghost following its master?"

The guru's eyes narrowed slightly, as though he was looking not at Gautam but into the fog itself

"Because, Gautam," he began slowly, "death is the one enemy that cannot be defeated. Every hunger can be satisfied, every wound can heal, every sorrow can pass. But death, death waits for all. And the mind knows this. That knowledge itself is the seed of fear."

Gautam shivered, though not only from the cold. "Then, Master, is all of man's misery born from this one fear?"

Brihaspati nodded. "Yes, much of it. Look at the temples rising in every village, the chants, the rituals."

"Look at poetry, at music, at tales of gods and afterlife. Do you think they are only for beauty? No".

"They are man's answer to death. He cannot stop death, so he builds meaning around it. He weaves songs, he paints, he dreams of heavens and rebirths. All so that death does not crush him."

The fog thickened, and Gautam could barely see the fields beyond.

He whispered, "So even religion, even art, are children of fear?"

The guru smiled faintly, a tired but gentle smile. "Yes. But fear is not only weakness. It is also strength."

"Fear of death makes man careful, it makes him value his life, protect his kin, and plan for the future."

"Without fear, man would walk into fire without thought. Fear keeps life burning, just as joy does. The two are brothers, one pushes forward, the other holds back. Together, they keep us alive."

For a while they both sat in silence, listening to the wind rush through the bare trees.

Gautam's face was thoughtful, his young eyes carrying both sorrow and wonder. He realized that even his longing for wisdom was tied to this same shadow, the wish to outlive death through knowledge.

At last, Brihaspati leaned on his knees and said softly, "Remember, Gautam. To live fully is not to escape death, but to walk with its shadow and still sing. That is what makes man different from all other creatures."

The mist swirled around them, and in its gray curtain, Gautam felt the words settle inside him like glowing embers, warming the cold morning from within.

Day 16

Survival of the Self, Ego, Identity, and the Will to Be Remembered

That evening the village had already begun lighting its lamps. The orange glow of fire torches flickered in the lanes, and the smell of woodsmoke drifted over the fields. The ashram courtyard felt warmer than the mornings, though the cold still pressed in from all sides.

Gautam could not sleep that night, his spent all night sitting with shawl wrapped tight.

Next day the sky above was clear for the first time in many days, cold mornings have a different shade of sky, one can always notice a different blue with changing seasons.

When Brihaspati arrived, his face carried a gentler look than yesterday. He lowered himself to the ground and placed his hands together as if to warm them on an invisible fire.

“Master,” Gautam began, his eyes glowing in the starlight, “yesterday you spoke of death’s shadow. I have thought since then, is it not true that even when we know our body will die, our mind refuses to accept it?”

“Is this why men created the idea of the aatmaa, the spirit that survives death?”

The guru smiled faintly, as If he had expected the question.

“Yes, Gautam, but listen carefully. What people call aatmaa, the spirit, is often misunderstood. The word aatmaa, came from misunderstanding the word aatman, which means the ‘self.’

Not a floating ghost or eternal soul, but the mind’s own picture of itself.

“Aatmaa is nothing but a psychological self, invented by mind for survival.”

The mind cannot bear to think that it will vanish. So it creates an image, an abstract ‘I’, that feels untouchable. This is the self, that mind protects day and night.”

Gautam leaned forward, his brows drawn. "So the aatman is not a divine spark? Not something given by the gods?"

Brihaspati shook his head slowly. "No, my child. It is the cleverest trick of the mind."

"Think, from childhood, the mind builds its own little fort. Inside that fort it places all that seems useful for survival. Toys in childhood, tools in youth, wealth in manhood, even friends and family, all are added to this aura of self."

You say, 'my toy, my tool, my wife, my son, my honor.' Each word of 'my' strengthens the walls of that fort."

"And finally, you begin to believe the fort itself is real, eternal, and must survive."

The firelight from the village shimmered faintly in the distance, making the guru's eyes shine.

Gautam whispered, almost to himself, "Then, Master, ego and self are the same fortress?"

"Yes," said Brihaspati. "The ego is only the gatekeeper of that fort. It guards the image, fights for it, feels wounded when the fort is attacked, and grows proud when the fort is praised."

"And yet, Gautam, this self is no solid jewel. It is only an idea, born from the survival instinct, yet floating like smoke."

For a moment, silence lay heavy between them. The day seemed endless, with only sparse clouds as their witness.

Then Gautam asked softly, "If the self is an illusion, why do we cling to it so fiercely?"

Brihaspati's gaze lifted to the sky, where the constellations shone like ancient fires.

"Because even illusions can save life, Gautam. The self gives courage, it gives purpose".

"It makes a man fight for his kin, for his name, for his honor. It keeps him alive longer than bare flesh alone could."

"Yet, when he mistakes it for eternal truth, misery follows. He then fears every insult as death, every loss as destruction of his very being."

Gautam sat still, his young face glowing with both wonder and unease.

He felt the words enter his chest like arrows, painful, but also awakening something hidden.

Brihaspati placed a hand on his shoulder, his voice low and warm, “Remember, the self is a raft, not the shore. Use it to cross life’s river”.

“But do not chain yourself to it. For when the river ends, the raft must be left behind.”

Gautam was so much into his thoughts that he didn’t realised, when the day slipped into dusk and dusk merged into night.

The stars glimmered brighter, and the smoke-scented air wrapped around them.

Gautam felt as if the forest itself was listening, storing these words for the ages.

Day 17

Wealth, Power, and War, Competition in Modern Disguise

Today the sun had risen sharp and cold. The air was still biting, but the sky was finally bright, washed clean after many days of fog.

Villagers were already moving in the distance, women carrying water pots on their heads, men driving their bullocks to the fields.

Their chatter mixed with the cries of crows that had returned after the silence of winter clouds.

Gautam sat outside the ashram, rubbing his palms together for warmth, his eyes squinting at the shining fields.

When Brihaspati arrived, he walked slowly but firmly, his bare feet leaving light marks on the cold earth.

His face was calm, though his gaze carried something sharp, like the sunlight itself.

"Master," Gautam said, bowing lightly, "yesterday you taught me about the self, the fortress built by the mind. I could not sleep much last night. For I kept asking, why is man never satisfied?"

"Even after food, after family, after safety, man still wants more, gold, land, power. Why does he fight, even kill, when he already has enough to live?"

Brihaspati lowered himself onto the ground, drawing his shawl tight around his shoulders.

His eyes rested on a farmer in the distance, shouting at his oxen. Then he spoke, his voice slow and steady.

"Because, Gautam, man's hunger is endless. Food fills the stomach for a few hours, but wealth fills the illusion of self. Power feeds the ego, and war feeds the tribe's pride. These too are survival tricks, but painted in grander colours."

Gautam's eyes widened. "So wealth and power also come from the same root as thirst or fear?"

The guru nodded. "Yes. Look at the animals. The strongest bull pushes the others aside to guard the herd. The lion fights for territory. Even the smallest bird pecks another to keep its seed."

"Survival is always a contest."

In man, this contest has become polished. He no longer fights only with claws".

"He fights with coins, with armies, with crowns."

He paused, and his voice grew firmer, "Remember, Gautam, wealth is not just gold. It is tools, land, knowledge. Anything that makes life more secure. Power is not just a throne. It is the strength to command others, to bend their will. And war is only the loudest form of the same struggle, the tribe proving it must not vanish."

The morning breeze stirred, carrying with it the smell of dung fires from the village.

Gautam looked troubled, his young brow furrowed. “But, Master, if all this is survival, why does it cause so much pain? Wars kill, greed poisons the heart. Is survival not meant to protect life?”

Brihaspati’s eyes softened. He touched the cold earth beside him and said, “That is nature’s blind way.”

“Survival cares not for peace, only for persistence”.

“A man may burn a village, yet his tribe grows stronger. A king may kill thousands, yet his name is remembered”.

“Survival writes no laws of fairness, only of success.”

Gautam lowered his head, silent for a long moment.

The distant sounds of villagers, laughter, quarrels, the creak of bullock carts, drifted around them like an endless background song.

Finally, he whispered, “Then perhaps the worst of man also comes from his will to survive.”

Brihaspati looked at him with quiet approval. “You are learning, Gautam. The survival fire warms, but it also burns. Wealth, power, and war are only its modern clothes."

The sun climbed higher, and the morning slowly turned golden.

But in Gautam's heart, the lesson felt heavy, like a shadow that stretched far into the future.

Day 18

The New Survival Tools, Technology

(Yantra-Vidya)

The afternoon sun was soft, its warmth a welcome relief from the morning chill.

The village blacksmith's shop stood at the edge of the road, half open to the sky, with sparks flying each time his hammer struck the glowing iron.

The sharp ringing sound echoed through the air, mixing with the smell of smoke and hot metal.

Children watched from a distance, wide-eyed, as if some magic was being born on the anvil.

Gautam and Brihaspati sat on a low mud wall nearby. The guru's eyes followed the rhythm of the hammer, steady and powerful.

Gautam leaned forward eagerly, sensing that today's lesson would be different.

"Master," Gautam asked, "yesterday you spoke of wealth and power. But here I see men with no gold, no throne, yet with fire and iron they seem strong. Is this too part of survival?"

Brihaspati smiled faintly. "Yes, Gautam. This is the secret of man's rise. Look closely, tools are man's second body."

"Fire, wheel, plough, bow, all are extensions of his hands, his teeth, his strength. Without them, man is weaker than many beasts. With them, he rules the beasts."

The blacksmith paused to wipe sweat from his brow, then pressed the iron back into the fire.

The flames roared brighter, licking the metal like a hungry tongue. Gautam's eyes reflected the glow.

"So fire itself," Gautam whispered, "is like another survival tool for man?"

"Exactly," Brihaspati said. "When man first held fire, he gained warmth in winter, light in darkness, and protection from beasts."

"When he shaped stone into blades, his weak hands became sharp claws. When he built the wheel, his legs ran farther than any deer. Every tool is a step beyond the limits of flesh." he added, "it is survival stretched outward."

The air hummed with the blacksmith's hammer. A village woman walked by carrying a clay pot, glancing curiously at the teacher and his disciple sitting so close to the forge.

"But Master," Gautam said slowly, "if tools are part of survival, then will they not also grow without end?"

"Today we see iron, tomorrow something greater. Will man ever stop?"

Brihaspati's gaze grew distant. The sparks reflected in his old eyes as if showing hidden worlds.

"Man will not stop, Gautam. His hunger for survival will push him further, beyond stone, beyond iron, beyond what we can imagine."

"Each invention will answer one danger, but also bring new dangers."

"Fire cooks food, but also burns villages. The bow hunts deer, but also kills men.

Yantra-vidya (Technology) is a two edged sword, it is like fire itself, it warms and it burns."

A silence followed. Only the steady hammer spoke, shaping the glowing iron into something useful yet dangerous.

Gautam folded his hands on his knees. "So man is never content with his body alone. He is always building another body around himself, tools, houses, even kingdoms?"

The guru nodded. "Yes. Tools are man's outer skin. It is the armor he wears against death. But remember, Gautam, it is born of the same root as all else, the will to survive."

The blacksmith raised the finished blade, shining under the sun, sharp and alive.

Gautam shivered.

Not from cold, but from the weight of the thought.

That survival had no limit, and man's tools were only the beginning of an endless path.

Day 19

Survival of Ideas, Culture and Knowledge

The banyan tree spread its roots like a giant's arms, touching earth and air together. Oil lamps flickered in the distance, villagers had begun to settle in for the night. Smoke from cooking fires curled slowly upward, mixing with the scent of lentils and burning wood.

Brihaspati and Gautam sat under the tree, starting very late today, their cloaks wrapped tightly against the cold. The fire between them gave a dim glow, casting long shadows on the ground.

"Master," Gautam said softly, "yesterday you spoke of tools as man's armor."

"But I see something else among the people. They live by stories."

"One tells how gods made the rivers, another sings of heroes in battle, and all seem to believe these words as if they were iron. Are stories also tools?"

Brihaspati's face lit up with quiet pride. "Yes, Gautam. You see well. Stories are tools of the mind. They are seeds planted in thought, passed from one tongue to another.

A blade cuts flesh, but a story cuts deeper, it shapes how men live and die."

The wind stirred the banyan leaves. A group of children nearby played a game, singing rhymes they did not fully understand, yet repeating them with joy. Gautam watched them curiously.

"See those children?" the guru said. "Their song will outlive their voices. That is how ideas survive".

"A man's body dies, but his words can travel beyond him, carried by others."

"This is another kind of survival, beyond blood."

Gautam frowned in thought. "So even belief in gods, even rituals, are for survival?"

"Indeed," Brihaspati replied. "When men share a story, they share trust."

"When they believe in the same god, they fight together, not against each other".

"Belief becomes a bond, stronger than kinship. It makes the weak many into the strong one."

"Culture, Gautam, is survival woven with words."

The fire popped, sending sparks upward. One landed on Gautam's wool cloak, and he quickly brushed it away. His face glowed with excitement.

"Then master," he asked, "is not knowledge itself the greatest weapon? A spear can break, a wall can fall, but words, can they not live forever?"

Brihaspati leaned closer, his voice low. "Yes."

"Knowledge is survival in its purest form".

"A bow is lost when the hand that holds it dies. But the knowledge of how to make the bow, if taught to another, cannot die so easily."

"That is why the wise write, why they teach, why they sing. They are not saving themselves, Gautam. They are saving survival itself."

Above them, the night sky spread wide and starry.

The cold deepened, but Gautam felt warmth in his chest.

He looked up at the constellations, those ancient stories written in the sky, and wondered how many generations had already carried them, and how many more would still whisper their names.

Day 20

The Future of Survival

The sun was late in waking that morning. A pale light spread slowly across the misty fields, where drops of dew clung to the grass like tiny beads of glass.

The air was cold enough to bite the skin, yet the sky held a faint promise of warmth. Somewhere in the distance, a farmer's bullock-cart creaked along the path, its sound muffled in the fog.

Gautam sat near the dying embers of the night's fire, rubbing his palms together for warmth.

He had hardly slept, for his thoughts were restless.

He had followed the guru's lessons from the first spark of life to the strength of ideas, and now a question rose in his chest like a storm waiting to break.

When Brihaspati arrived, his steps were slow but steady. His face was calm, his breath misting in the cold air.

He lowered himself onto the mat, drew his woollen shawl close, and gazed at Gautam with the gentle patience of a river.

"Guru," Gautam said without greeting, his voice trembling with eagerness, "you have shown me how survival is the root of all, body, mind, family, society, even belief."

"But tell me, what is to come?"

"Are we forever bound to this chain of survival? Or will mankind one day rise beyond it?"

Brihaspati smiled faintly, as though the question had waited long in his own heart. He picked up a small twig and began to draw circles in the soft earth.

"Gautam, survival is the first law of life. Without it, nothing can be built."

"Yet man is strange, he dreams not only of living, but of living beyond. He makes palaces when a hut would do, he seeks gold when grain is enough, he imagines gods when silence is sufficient. This is his strength, and his misery."

The fog shifted, a shaft of sunlight broke through, touching the guru's hand. He looked at it quietly.

"Perhaps one day," he continued, "man may learn to master even his own instincts.

To eat not from hunger, but for health.

To fight not from fear, but for justice.

To believe not in gods, but in truth itself.

“That day will be the true future of survival, not the end of it, but its flowering.”

Gautam’s eyes widened, his breath quickened. “So you mean, master, that even when we go beyond survival, we are still within it?”

“Just so,” Brihaspati said, tapping the twig against the ground. “A tree is rooted in earth, but its branches touch the sky.”

“Man’s root is survival. But what he grows into, that is his choice, his destiny. If he does not grow, he will perish like the forgotten species before him. If he grows, perhaps he will shape a world where survival is no longer a fear, but a foundation for higher life.”

For a long moment, both sat in silence.

The fog was lifting, and the calls of birds returned, faint but rising.

Gautam felt as if the whole world was breathing with him, as if he, too, was a branch reaching upward.

At last he whispered, “Master, then the question is not only how to survive, but how to live.”

Brihaspati's eyes shone in the morning light. "Yes, Gautam. That is the last lesson."

Day 21

The Departure

The night before was long, and sleep never touched Gautam's eyes.

He sat through the hours of darkness like a stone, unmoving, his breath shallow but steady, as though he were carved from the silence itself.

No fire burned beside him, no bird called, no wind stirred. He was alone, yet not empty, his mind was alive, replaying each of the twenty days gone by.

He saw again the first spark of conversation, when his guru had spoken of chance and survival.

He heard again the words on fear, hunger, love, and death.

He felt again the weight of the questions about gods and self, the restless longing of the mind to outlive the body.

Each day stood before him like a page, and he turned them one by one, as if stitching together a book inside his heart.

When dawn came, Gautam did not rise.

When the sun crossed the sky, still he did not move.

He waited. He waited as if the waiting itself was the final lesson.

It was almost evening when Brihaspati appeared.

The guru's steps were slow, his shawl wrapped close against the sharp December air. He said nothing at first. He simply stood before Gautam, watching his disciple who sat still as a mountain.

At last, Gautam spoke, his voice low, almost breaking.

"Master, twenty-one days have passed. I have learned how life fights to live, how every bond is born from survival, how even the gods are shadows of our longing."

"But tell me, what shall I do with this learning? Should I return as a king, to rule and command? Or should I live as an ordinary man, learning and teaching, free from the burdens of the throne?"

Brihaspati's face was calm, but his eyes carried a gentle fire.

"You ask not what you have learned, Gautam, but what you must become."

"That is a question no teacher can answer for you."

"Rule, if ruling does not blind you to the root of life."

"Live as a man, if you can bear the simplicity. Or do both, for the world often demands one while the soul longs for the other."

Gautam lowered his head. "And will this knowledge make me a better king? Or only a troubled one?"

The guru's lips curved into the faintest smile.

"A better king is one who knows he is a man before he is a king. A better man is one who knows he is only a spark before he is a man. If you remember this, Gautam, then neither throne nor poverty can trap you. You will be free, even when bound."

The air grew colder as the sun dipped.

Crows flew across the sky, their cries breaking the stillness.

The ashram looked quiet, timeless, as though it too was watching this farewell.

Gautam rose slowly. His body was stiff, his heart heavy, yet his mind was strangely light. He bowed deeply.

"Master, I came as a prince. I leave as, I do not know what. Perhaps that is your gift to me."

Brihaspati placed a hand on his shoulder.

For a moment, the old charvaka guru, Brahaspati, the hard-core materialist, who spoke always of earth and never of heaven, looked almost like a father bidding farewell to his son.

"Go, Gautam. Whether you rule or wander, whether you live for crown or for wisdom, remember this, life survives, and in survival, it becomes more. The rest is your choice."

As the last light faded, Gautam turned toward the road that would take him back to his kingdom.

Each step carried a question, Will I rule? Will I renounce? Will I ever be the same?

Yet, deep within, he felt something certain, a quiet fire, and a clarity that no crown or burden could extinguish.

The twenty-one days had ended.

But the journey had only begun.

www.ingramcontent.com/pod-product-compliance
Ingram Content Group UK Ltd.
Pitfield, Milton Keynes, MK11 3LW, UK
UKHW021409190726
13845UKWH00028B/986

9 789334 405002